INGER and LASSE SANDBERG

Translated by Judy Abbott Maurer

Dusty
Wants to Borrow
Everything

R&S
BOOKS

Stockholm   New York   Toronto   London   Adelaide

Rabén & Sjögren Stockholm

Text copyright © 1984 by Inger Sandberg
Illustrations copyright © 1984 by Lasse Sandberg
Translation copyright © 1988 by Judy Abbott Maurer
All rights reserved
Library of Congress catalog card number: 87-27253
Originally published in Sweden under the title
Låna den, sa Pulvret by Rabén & Sjögren, 1984
Printed in Italy 1988
First published in the United Kingdom 1988
First American edition, 1988

ISBN 91 29 58782 4

R&S Books are distributed in the United States of America by Farrar, Straus and Giroux, New York;
in the United Kingdom by Ragged Bears, Andover; in Canada by Methuen Publications, Toronto, Ontario;
and in Australia by ERA Publications, Adelaide

Dusty is spending the day
with Grandma and Grandpa.
"Let's go inside," says Grandpa.

"**Borrow this?**" asks Dusty right away
and reaches for Grandpa's **hat.**

"Yes, you may borrow my hat," says Grandpa.
"Dusty looks **nice**," says Dusty.

Dusty sees other things he would like to have.
"Borrow this?" asks Dusty,
as he pulls off Grandma's **glasses.**

"You may borrow my **old** glasses instead,"
Grandma says.
"I need to wear my new glasses,
or I can't see."

In the kitchen there are many things to borrow.
"Borrow this?" asks Dusty.
But Grandpa jumps forward and takes the knife.
"When you are **big**, you may use the knife," he says.

"You may borrow the **wooden spoon** instead."
"Not **that**," says Dusty
and points at the knife.
"That's right," says Grandpa.

"**Borrow this?**" asks Dusty.
He points at Grandma's **watch.**
"No, **not** the watch," says Grandma.
"Borrow this!" cries Dusty with a very sad face.

"All right, you may borrow my watch for a **little** while," says Grandma.
Dusty is happy.

In the hall Dusty sees a **hockey shirt.**
He pulls it down.
"Borrow this?" asks Dusty.
But it's so **hard** to put on the shirt!
Everything goes **wrong.**
Dusty is so **angry** that he begins to **shout.**

Grandpa helps Dusty.
"There, Dusty, now you look **nice**."

Dusty is not satisfied yet.

"Borrow these?" asks Dusty
as he steps into Grandpa's big shoes.

Dusty is **pleased.**
The shoes make a lot of **noise** when he walks.

Dusty clomps into Grandma's room.
Suddenly it is very **quiet.**
Just then, Dusty's mama arrives.
"Where's my little boy?" she asks.
"He is probably sleeping," says Grandpa.
"I can't **believe** that," says Mama.

Mama looks into Grandma's room.
"Who's that?" she cries.
Mama doesn't recognize her own son
because Dusty has on Grandpa's **hat**
and Grandma's old **glasses**
and Grandma's **watch**
and the **hockey shirt**
and Grandpa's big **shoes.**
Dusty is clutching the **wooden spoon,**
and tangled all around him
is Grandma's **yarn.**

"Borrow everything," says Dusty
when Mama tries to untangle him.
"It's nice to have you visit, Dusty,"
say Grandma and Grandpa,
"but now we need to rest.
You can come see us another day."